TIM HANKINSON has been a head coach for 40 years. He has coached in Major League Soccer, NASL, USL, India I-League, Guatemala U-17 National Team, Iceland and Jamaica professional leagues. His collegiate career spans five Universities and appeared in the 1980 and 1981 NCAA Final Fours. Soccer has taken his adventures around the world. Tim has been named NASL Coach of the Year, USISL Coach of the Year, Big East Coach of the Year and Iceland's FIFA Fair Play recipient.

I dedicate The Adventures of Plato to my children and my wife Yvette who have held up our home and family to allow me to follow my dream of coaching the beautiful game. "Thank you! and I love you all!!"

Go For Greatness!

THE ADVENTURES OF PLATO

Hi my name is 'Plato'!

You say it like "plah-toh"

I am a soccer cone.

In Spanish they call soccer cones "platos" because we are the shape of plates.

I LIKE MY NAME SO CALL ME PLATO!

Meet my best friend Tango! He is a "pelota de fútbol" or soccer ball! He loves to score goals. We are both very important to soccer practice, games, and developing skills.

More skills means more fun! Come join us in our soccer adventures!

2¡VAMONOS! LET'S GO!

The coach blows his whistle, "Tweet..Tweet" and points to the incoming dark clouds. "A storm is coming," the coach tells the players. "We need to collect the cones and balls quickly!" As some players collect the equipment around the field, Plato tells them, "Great practice!" But most players are too busy running to their parent's cars for safety.

3

OH NO WE LEFT PLATO!

Tango knew right away Plato was gone.
His best friend had been left behind.

He was very sad, but determined to
find Plato someday. He promised.

'I WILL NEVER GIVE UP, I WILL
NEVER QUIT LOOKING FOR PLATO!'

4

Plato was all alone... The rain poured down and the lightning cracked. Plato was frightened and shivered through the dark scary night.

"Why was I left behind?" Plato wondered.

The morning sun warmed Plato and the blue sky made him smile. But he still wondered where his team was and why he was left behind.

This made Plato sad. Suddenly the roar of a bus stopped at the soccer field.

Yay! It was a soccer team coming to practice. But not just any team! It was the National Team from Mexico, "El Tri".

Plato was very happy.

6

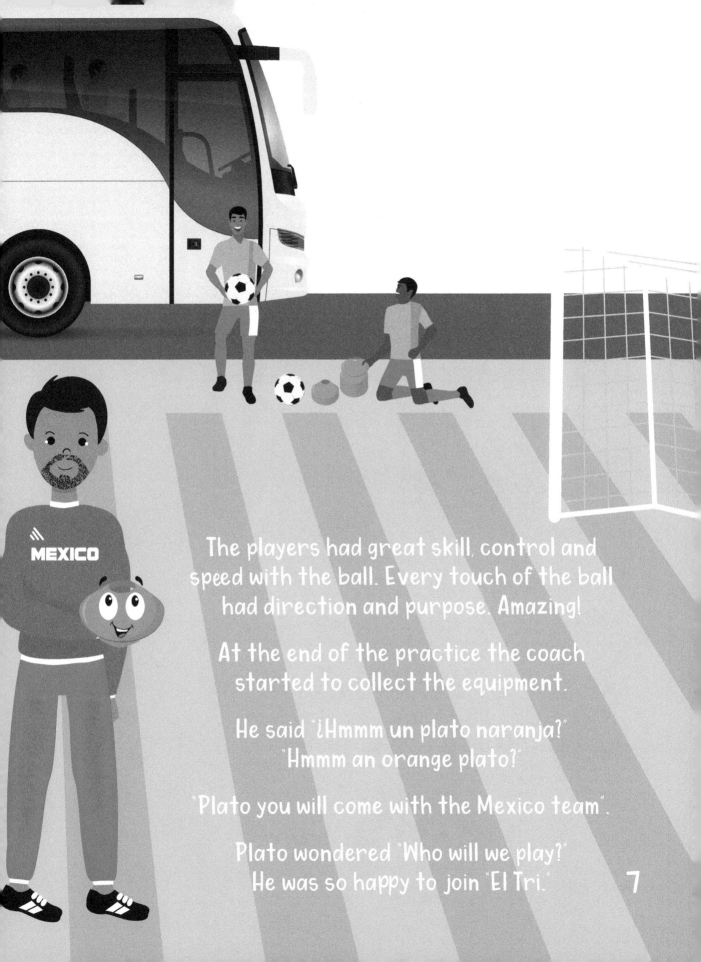

The players had great skill, control and speed with the ball. Every touch of the ball had direction and purpose. Amazing!

At the end of the practice the coach started to collect the equipment.

He said "¿Hmmm un plato naranja?" "Hmmm an orange plato?"

"Plato you will come with the Mexico team".

Plato wondered "Who will we play?" He was so happy to join "El Tri."

Today the Mexican National Team has a game at the stadium. Their fans all chant

"Ole' Ole' Ole'"

But wait! Oh my!! We are playing against the United States National Team! Their fans cheer

"USA USA USA"

"Who will I cheer for?" wonders Plato.

"I wish Tango was here to watch the game between the two big rival teams.

I will cheer for both teams to play an exciting game with teamwork, skill, fair play, and GOOOAAALLLSSS!"

POW!

Ole' Ole' Ole' USA USA USA!

The players warm up with dynamic stretches and movement, agility, passing and possession games. The coach has placed me into the drills to help guide the players.

The stadium and fans are so exciting.

LET'S PLAY!

We are ready! ¡Listos! 9

The referee blows the whistle. He is in charge and the game begins!
"The players are so fast and pass the ball so quickly," thinks Plato.

A shot on goal from each team brings the fans to their feet.
"Ole' Ole' Ole'" "USA USA USA" chants competing in the stadium
by the fans trying to encourage their teams to get a goal!

Plato observes from the bench the way the players control
the ball with their first touch. They already know where to
play the ball before they receive it. It's Amazing!

If I could only share what
I am learning with my old team.
I wish they were here with Tango

Suddenly a shot on goal into the corner of the net

Goooaaalll for Mexico! 'Ole' Ole' Ole'! The stadium is full of excitement.
The fans are standing, jumping and singing! With only minutes left in
the game, the USA players counter-attack sending a cross in
front of the goal. The American player jumps as high as he
can to head the ball into the net past the
Mexican goalkeeper.

"USA USA USA!" chant
the American fans.

USA

USA

USA

The referee blows his whistle three times signaling the game has ended. The teams have tied, USA 1-1 Mexico!

Both teams shake hands in "Fair Play" and many exchange their game jerseys as a memory of the match between two great rivals. These two great teams will compete and play another day to prepare for the 2026 World Cup.

Plato realizes he has seen a great game and is impressed how the players gave their best every minute of the match. Plato thinks "Bring your best every day! That is how you become a winner!"

13

The morning after the game, the coach from Mexico took the balls and cones to set up for a practice for the players before they fly back to Mexico.

This training is to help the players recover from the match. The players will start with different movements to let their muscles warm-up. Then they will stop a number of times for Dynamic stretching.

After stretching the team plays a game of "Keep away" called Rondo. Plato loves being a part of the action! The players then went to play some soccer tennis to have fun and relax.

"The players are not relaxing! They try to win at everything they do!" says Plato.

14

The practice is over and the coach asks the players to help pick up balls and cones. Plato smiles because his old team likes to help the coach as well. Then Plato hears voices walking towards the field. He hears the voice of his best friend Tango yelling "It's Plato, we have to get Plato!".

Plato is excited to see his old team.
The coaches meet and greet each other.

"¡Hola!"
says the coach of Mexico

"Hello!"
says the coach of Plato's team

All the cones from the Mexico team are blue. Plato stands out because he is orange. The coaches shake hands and the Mexico coach gladly returns Plato to his old team.

With big smiles both teams wave and wish each other

"¡Buena suerte!", and "Good luck!"

15

Plato had never been happier than he was to see his team and Tango! The coach blew his whistle to start the practice.

Warm up, dribbling with speed and passing started the practice. Then the coach tells the team to play a 1-2 pass around Plato and shoot to goal!

Tango was dribbled by one of our players towards Plato. Then played a 1-2 pass around him and took the shot kicking Tango with power into the upper corner!

All the players celebrated a great goal! Plato and Tango were back together helping the players develop their skills. "More skill equals more fun" said the coach. "Good practice! Everyone collect the balls and cones" "Be on time for our game tomorrow! Remember to bring uniforms, shin guards, soccer socks and cleats with your water bottle, so we are ready to play hard as a TEAM!"

Plato and Tango smiled with happiness because they now know, no-one gets left behind!

It is game day! The players are in uniform ready for the whistle to start the game. He is watching his best friend Tango who is the game ball today. Tango is ready for kickoff!

Plato is so proud of Tango and cheers for him "Go Tango Go!". Plato remembered the USA vs Mexico game and how hard the teams played, but also the Fair Play shown by the players and coaches.

Plato yells to his team "Play with speed, skill and as a team!"

"This is the greatest sport ever" thinks Plato.

What a beautiful game.
Qué hermoso juego.

THE END

PLATO DRILLS AND TANGO SKILLS:
First Touch and Passing

These are practices to help you develop your first touch and passing skills. It is important you learn to touch the ball when you receive it, taking the ball in a new direction. You will find this ability will help you play fast, direct the attack in a new direction and escape pressuring defenders.

Never stop the ball, always keep it moving!

Drill #1. In the first practice each player stands behind a cone. Player A passes Tango from the side of the cone to player B. Player B will not stop the ball, but will touch the ball to the right side of the cone opening a new passing lane to play the next pass back to player A. Player A slides over to the new channel to receive the pass. Player A's first touch directs Tango to the right side of the cone and returns a pass into a new channel for Player B.

Set-up: Cones are 7-10 yards distance.

Time: Play the First touch passing game for 60 seconds.

Recovery: 30 seconds and reverse direction.

Repetitions: 4 total minutes. Two minutes to the right and two minutes to the left. This is a daily exercise to become so comfortable with first touch that the players keep their vision up rather than down at a players feet.

Drill #2. In the second practice players start on the opposite side of each cone. Use the same set up and the same first touch to change direction with Tango. But now add a diagonal pass to split Plato and the other cone. Continue to shuffle across to the other side to give each other passing angles and support.

Time: 60 seconds one direction.
60 seconds reverse direction. Repeat.

Recovery: 30 Seconds

Reps: 4 total minutes. This is a daily exercise.

Drill #1   Drill #2

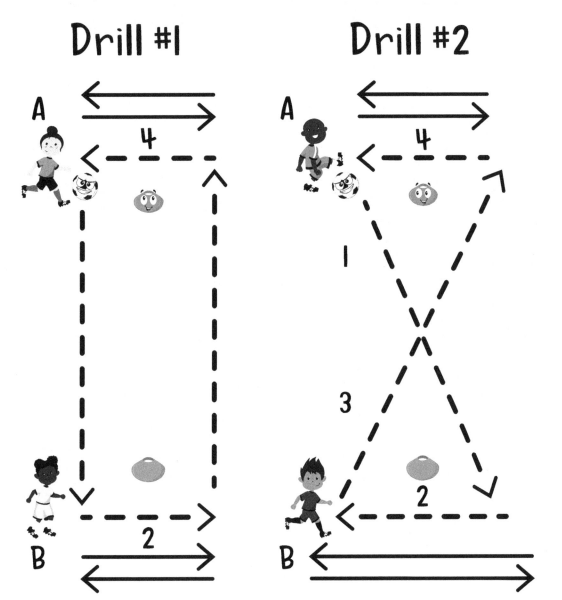

GLOSSARY

SPANISH WORDS AND EXPRESSIONS:

1. Buena Suerte - Good Luck
2. 'El Tri' - The three colors in the Mexican flag used as a nickname for the Mexico National Team
3. Listos - Ready
4. Ole' Ole' Ole' or USA USA USA - Fans chanting and cheering
5. Pelota de Fútbol - Soccer Ball
6. Plato - Name of a plate. Similar shape to a soccer cone
7. Plato Naranja - Orange Cone
8. Qué hermoso juego - What a Beautiful Game
9. Rondo - Small games that quicken skills and decision making
10. Vamanos - Let's Go!

ENGLISH WORDS AND EXPRESSIONS:

11. 1-2's - The player with the ball passes to a teammate who returns the pass
12. 2026 World Cup - Every four years 32 National Teams qualify to play in the biggest tournament in the World to become Champions. In 2026 The World Cup will be hosted by the USA, Mexico, and Canada
13. Counter Attack - After winning the ball a team runs into the attack with speed towards goal
14. Cross - Kicking the ball from the side of the goal area towards the front of the goal trying to score. Often players use their head to direct the cross towards the goal
15. Dynamic Stretching - Warming up and stretching the muscles with movement
16. Fair Play - Respect for the other team and referee while following the rules
17. Goalkeeper - The only player on each team that can use their hands. The job of the GK is to stop the ball from scoring a goal
18. Referee - Controls the game by making sure both teams follow the rules
19. Rivals - Two teams that play very hard against each other to win the game
20. Shot - Kicking the ball to score a goal
21. USA National Team and Mexican National Team - The best professional players that are selected to represent their country in International competition

CPSIA information can be obtained
at www.ICGtesting.com
Printed in the USA
LVHW071355090221
678830LV00010B/85